Samir's Best Sports Day

by Elizabeth Dale and Art Gus

W
FRANKLIN WATTS
LONDON • SYDNEY

Samir was excited. It was Sports Day at school and he really, really wanted to win a race. But he wasn't sure he was good enough. He never won anything at Sports Day.

2

Samir lined up with other children at the start of the egg and spoon race, clutching his spoon tightly. The egg wobbled on the spoon.

He was worried that it would fall off as soon as
he started running. He looked over at his mum.
She smiled at him and gave him a thumbs-up.
He felt a bit better.

When Mr Simms blew the whistle,

Samir started running.

But almost at once he dropped the egg.

Samir picked it up quickly and carried on.

But he dropped the egg again and he was

the last to cross the line. He was very upset.

"Never mind, Samir," said Mr Simms.

"You tried hard."

Next it was the high jump. Samir gazed

at the bar. It seemed very high.

Samir watched as Izzy jumped over it.

But when Samir jumped, he knocked off
the bar.

Afterwards, Samir clapped
as the other children jumped over the bar.

"Maybe I'll win this race?" thought Samir

as he lined up for the dressing up race.

After all, he was good at getting dressed

quickly. He did it every morning.

Mr Simms had put lots of dressing up clothes
on the track. As soon as the whistle went,
Samir ran to the big floppy hat and put it on.
Then he put on the baggy trousers. But he was
in such a rush that he didn't do up the button.

He hadn't got far when the trousers fell down
and tripped him up.

Samir got up and ran again, holding
his trousers. But he could not catch up.

Everyone clapped when he came last.

But Samir could not smile.

Mr Simms did not like to see Samir look sad.

"Well done for trying, Samir," said Mr Simms.

"Now, can you help me, please?

I need someone to take some photos of today

for our school newsletter and website.

Could you do that for me?"

Samir looked a bit worried. "I can try," he said.

Samir loved taking the photos.

He took one of Anna doing a very long jump.

Then it was the running race. Samir planned

to take a photo of the winner crossing the line.

But just as Mr Simms blew his whistle, Samir realised he was at the starting line, not the finishing line.

He ran as fast as he could to the finishing line and just managed to take a photo of Max crossing the line ahead of the others.

Samir was surprised when Mr Simms gave him a gold winner's sticker.

"Well done, Samir," Mr Simms said. "You were at the start when the whistle went and you were first to cross the line. So you were the fastest."

Samir smiled. He had won a race, just like he wanted. The crowd cheered and clapped – and his mum cheered loudest of all.

Samir wore his gold sticker proudly as he took more photos. He took a photo of Lucy laughing as she threw her javelin backwards by mistake.

He took a photo of Simon making a funny face as he wobbled on his stilts and fell off.

He took a photo of Lisa giggling when she tripped up in the sack race.

None of them won a race or were given
a gold sticker. But they were all having fun.
And as he took their photos, Samir realised that
having fun was what mattered most of all.
It was his best Sports Day ever!

Story order

Look at these 5 pictures and captions.
Put the pictures in the right order
to retell the story.

1

Samir came last in the egg and spoon race.

2

Samir came first in the running race.

3

Samir came last in the dressing up race.

4

Samir was excited about Sports Day.

5

Mr Simms asked Samir to take photos.

Independent Reading

This series is designed to provide an opportunity for your child to read on their own. These notes are written for you to help your child choose a book and to read it independently.

In school, your child's teacher will often be using reading books which have been banded to support the process of learning to read. Use the book band colour your child is reading in school to help you make a good choice. *Samir's Best Sports Day* is a good choice for children reading at Gold Band in their classroom to read independently.

The aim of independent reading is to read this book with ease, so that your child enjoys the story and relates it to their own experiences.

About the book

Samir is very excited about Sports Day and he really hopes to win a race. But nothing goes to plan and he ends up finishing last in every one. Then Mr Simms asks him to take some photos, and Samir's day gets much better!

Before reading

Help your child to learn how to make good choices by asking: "Why did you choose this book? Why do you think you will enjoy it?" Look at the cover together and ask: "What do you think the story will be about?" Ask your child to think of what they already know about Sports Day. Then ask your child to read the title aloud. Ask: "Do you think Samir is going to enjoy Sports Day at school?" Remind your child that they can sound out the letters to make a word if they get stuck.

Decide together whether your child will read the story independently or read it aloud to you.

During reading

Remind your child of what they know and what they can do independently. If reading aloud, support your child if they hesitate or ask for help by telling the word. If reading to themselves, remind your child that they can come and ask for your help if stuck.

After reading

Support comprehension by asking your child to tell you about the story. Use the story order puzzle to encourage your child to retell the story in the right sequence, in their own words. The correct sequence can be found on the next page.

Help your child think about the messages in the book that go beyond the story and ask: "How do you think Samir felt when he did not win the races? Why do you think Mr Simms asked Samir to take the photos?"

Give your child a chance to respond to the story: "Have you ever taken part in Sports Day? Did you enjoy it?"

Extending learning

Help your child predict other possible outcomes of the story by asking: "If Mr Simms had not asked Samir to take the photos, what might have happened? Do you think Samir would have enjoyed Sports Day?"

In the classroom, your child's teacher may be teaching contractions. There are many examples in this book that you could look at together, including *I'll* (I will), *wasn't* (was not), *didn't* (did not), *hadn't* (had not). Find these together and point out how the apostrophes are used in place of the omitted letters.

Franklin Watts
First published in Great Britain in 2020
by The Watts Publishing Group

Series Editors: Jackie Hamley and Melanie Palmer
Series Advisors: Dr Sue Bodman and Glen Franklin
Series Designers: Peter Scoulding and Cathryn Gilbert

A CIP catalogue record for this book is
available from the British Library.

ISBN 978 1 4451 6940 8 (hbk)
ISBN 978 1 4451 6941 5 (pbk)
ISBN 978 1 4451 7310 8 (library ebook)

Printed in China

Franklin Watts
An imprint of
Hachette Children's Group
Part of The Watts Publishing Group
Carmelite House
50 Victoria Embankment
London EC4Y 0DZ

An Hachette UK Company
www.hachette.co.uk

www.reading-champion.co.uk

For Summer –
the inspiration for this
story – who was a brilliant
photographer when
she wasn't well enough
to take part in Sports Day
– E.D.

Answer to Story order: 4, 1, 3, 5, 2